"I couldn't believe it. There it was, right in front of me, an empty pool just waiting for me to skate it."

KEVIN SIMON

Age: 13
Hometown: A town in Ohio
that you've never heard of

STONE ARCH BOOKS
presents

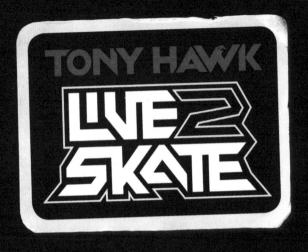

STRONG

written by

MATTHEW K. MANNING

images by

FERNANDO CANO and **JOE AZPEYTIA**

a
CAPSTONE
production

Published by Stone Arch Books
A Capstone Imprint
1710 Roe Crest Drive, North Mankato, Minnesota 56003
www.capstonepub.com • www.capstoneyoungreaders.com

Printed in the United States of America in Stevens Point,
Wisconsin.   032013   007227WZF13

Library of Congress Cataloging-in-Publication Data is
available on the Library of Congress website.
Hardcover: 978-1-4342-4085-9
Paperback: 978-1-4342-6187-8

Summary: Kevin isn't happy to be helping the neighbor, until
he finds an empty pool, perfect for skating.

Designer: Bob Lentz
Creative Director: Heather Kindseth

Design Elements: Shutterstock.

CHAPTERS

COMMITTED

"Here, man. Spray the top of his head like this," Duke said. He swirled the can of red spray paint in the air so Kevin would know what he meant. As if Kevin didn't understand how spray paint worked.

"Okay, okay," Kevin said. He took the can and climbed up onto the base of the statue. He paused for a second. He was committed now. This was happening whether he wanted it to or not.

Kevin Simon looked at the life-size statue in front of him. He wasn't even sure who this old guy was. Maybe he was a former mayor or senator or something. Kevin couldn't be sure. He'd have to look it up when he got home.

"Let's go, man. Make him into Santa," Duke said from the grass surrounding the statue's base. "The cops could show up any second." Duke could tell that Kevin was lost in thought, and it bothered him.

Duke wasn't really a big thinker. And what's more, he didn't care much for anyone who was. After all, this situation was pretty cut and dried. You take the can of spray paint, give the old man statue a Santa Claus hat, and maybe some creepy Joker-like smile, and get out of there before they all ended up in juvie.

"You want me to show you again?" asked Duke. Kevin ignored him.

Duke looked over at Billy Pit for support. Billy was nothing if not Duke's number one cheerleader. He had been there to back Duke up since kindergarten, and he never seemed to mind.

They were the kind of friends that didn't look like they had much in common at first glance. Billy was a good two heads taller than Duke. He was cleaner cut, preferring neat, straight jeans and sneakers that always looked like they had been purchased yesterday. Duke, on the other hand, wore baggy jeans and old shoes that seemed to be on the verge of busting open at the toe. Billy was black, and his short, buzzed hair looked the opposite of Duke's long, blond surfer locks that fell over his pale, white skin.

Nevertheless, the two had been inseparable since they first met. Billy seemed to go along with every single bad idea Duke could cook up. And tonight was no exception. Spray-painting a statue right in the middle of the town square wasn't high on Billy's to-do list. But there he was anyway.

"Yeah, man," Billy said. "Hurry it up."

"You were the one who wanted to tag along," Duke said to Kevin. "Get it done already, man. Stop being such a wuss."

While he was slightly taller than Duke, Kevin was fairly short for his age. So he had to stand on his tiptoes and stretch his arm up as far as it would go to reach the statue's top. He pressed his finger down on the nozzle and emptied way too much of the can onto the old man's head. Streams of paint flowed down the statue's temples and into its eyes. Red tears dripped down its stone cheeks. The end result didn't look much like Santa Claus at all.

"Ha!" Duke said. "Now give him, like, lipstick or something."

Kevin looked down at Duke and Billy, then back up at the statue. His hair fell into his eyes. He pushed it back with his hand, and then he pointed the spray paint at the statue's mouth.

"Hey!" a deep voice called out.

All three of the boys turned at the sound of the voice. A police officer was quickly running their way.

"Stop right there!" he shouted.

Duke and Billy shot off toward the nearby curb where they had left their skateboards a few minutes ago. Kevin heard the familiar sound of polyurethane wheels hitting pavement, followed by the squeak of Billy's new shoes. He jumped down off the base of the statue and followed his friends. They were already a good block ahead of him. Kevin had some serious catching up to do.

He stepped on his board and pushed hard. He shot off across the street and onto the nearby sidewalk. There was no need to look back at the cop. He could hear the man panting behind him clearly enough. Even though he sounded out of

breath, the police officer was gaining on him. Kevin pushed harder. There was no time for any fancy tricks. All that mattered now was speed.

The guys were no longer in sight. They'd turned down a street a few blocks away and were heading for the park near Billy's house. But Kevin knew how to catch up to them. He'd take the alley by McCrory's drugstore. All he had to do was turn on Fifth Street. He'd be safely hidden in Billy's basement before he knew it.

Making the corner was easy enough. Kevin slid smoothly past the lamppost, avoiding a large crack in the pavement. Feeling confident, he took a second to look over his shoulder. The cop was a block behind him now. This was actually going to work. Once he hit the alley, he'd be home free.

But when Kevin turned back around to look where he was going, it wasn't the alley that he saw in front of him. Instead, a large man in a blue uniform stood there, blocking his way.

Kevin swerved to the right, but it was too late. The cop grabbed him by the arm and pulled him clear off his board.

"I believe my partner asked you to stop," the officer said in a calm tone. Kevin watched his skateboard coast down the block toward the alleyway. At least one of them was going to make a clean getaway.

PUNISHMENT

Mr. Belmont was just trying to read his book. He didn't think that was too much to ask. After all, he was sitting on a bench outside the local library. In his opinion, there were very few areas in this small Ohio town where reading was more appropriate. He had been enjoying this comfortable spot under the town's gazebo for the better part of the last six decades. But today that wasn't quite the case. Because across the large gazebo from Mr. Belmont were two kids who looked like they had never cracked open a book in their lives.

"No, man, a *crooked* grind," the blond boy said to his friend. "Gotta point it down."

"That's what I did," said the tall boy with the deep voice.

The smaller of the two threw his board on the concrete floor of the large gazebo. The sound made Mr. Belmont's shoulders jump. He immediately regretted his reaction. His plan was to ignore these rude kids completely. He didn't want to give them the satisfaction of knowing that they were bothering him.

Mr. Belmont tried to find his place on the page he was reading. He started the paragraph over.

"Like this," the smaller boy yelled from across the gazebo. Mr. Belmont didn't look up. From the noise, it sounded as if the boy's attempt at whatever a crooked grind was had failed miserably. Then Mr. Belmont felt a sudden discomfort in his foot. He looked down to see that the boy's skateboard had shot across the floor and collided with his own shoe. His focus shifted up to the boy sitting on the concrete in front of him. The kid was laughing wildly. His friend was smiling as well. Mr. Belmont did not share their amusement.

He stood up and brushed his thin, brown pants to straighten them. Then he walked away from the boys toward the stairs. He looked at the young, blond boy as he went. The boy looked away, pretending he didn't see the old man.

He didn't even have the decency to make eye contact. Mr. Belmont grunted a bit under his breath as he walked toward his car in the nearby parking lot.

* * *

Kevin heard Duke and Billy before he actually saw them. He was walking out of the library with his mom when he heard Duke's high-pitched cackle. It had been about a month since the incident with the statue. In that time, Kevin had been forbidden to talk to his skater friends. His mom thought they were bad influences, and she was probably right.

While the town hadn't pressed charges, Kevin's first venture into the world of vandalism had angered his parents. He was told he was going to be punished, but then nothing happened. It was as if his parents enjoyed making him sweat it out. They wanted him to worry about what his punishment was going to be. They wanted him constantly wondering when the other shoe would drop.

Kevin didn't want his mom to see him with his friends, but he was far more concerned that the guys would see the huge stack of books he was carrying. Kevin was an avid reader, although he kept that fact a carefully guarded secret. When not skating, his free time wasn't spent on other sports or video games. It was spent on the torn, old, green recliner in the corner of his bedroom. There he would hunch over the latest sci-fi novel or some historical adventure.

While he loved reading, he didn't love the ridicule that sometimes came along with it. The guys already thought of him as some kind of boy scout. Kevin didn't need to make it worse than it already was.

So the plan was simple. Kevin Simon was going to make his way across the parking lot as quickly as possible. Then he'd hide in the back of the SUV until his mom started driving and they were a few blocks away. The guys were all the way across the lot in the gazebo. They wouldn't see him if he ducked down behind the row of cars. That is, as long as Kevin's mom could keep up the pace.

Then Kevin heard the worst possible sentence that could come from his mom's mouth at that particular moment. "Hold on a second, honey," she said. He turned to argue, but his mom was already walking away from him, headed toward the other end of the parking lot. She was approaching an old man with gray hair, a matching polo shirt, and brown pants. Kevin recognized the man right away. It was his neighbor, Mr. Belmont.

Mr. Belmont lived on the large plot of land behind Kevin's house in the country. Kevin's home was firmly planted in the boonies, as his dad liked to call it. They were a five-minute car ride from town, and Mr. Belmont was one of the only neighbors within walking distance.

Even though they were neighbors, Kevin didn't know the old man very well. He remembered getting big bags of candy at Mr. Belmont's house on Halloween when he was younger. And he remembered seeing Mr. Belmont at a Christmas party a few years ago. But other than that, the old guy seemed to keep to himself. So Kevin wasn't sure why his mom was in such a hurry to talk to him today.

Regardless, Kevin was still trying to hide. Whether his mom was in on his plan or not, he was going to make it to that SUV unseen. He ducked his head down and made a beeline for the car. He walked quickly, or as quickly as he could manage without spilling his stack of books. He could

hear the sounds of Duke and Billy's boards clacking against the gazebo's floor and handrail. The guys hadn't noticed him yet.

Finally, he made it to the SUV and let himself look up toward the gazebo. He couldn't see Duke, but he spotted Billy looking in the other direction. That was a good sign. Kevin tried the handle on the SUV's back door. It didn't budge. The car was locked. He looked back behind him at his mom. She was still talking to Mr. Belmont. What could they be going on about? How long did she plan on making him wait out there?

Kevin put the stack of books down on the ground. He crouched down beside them so as not to be visible between the parked cars. He couldn't even stash the books inside the SUV. There was nothing he could do but wait.

"Yo, Simon. Are you building a fort out of books or what?" Duke said from behind him. Both Kevin and Billy always called Kevin by his last name. For some reason they thought it sounded cooler than saying "Kevin." He wasn't sure why, especially since Simon could be a first name, too.

Kevin turned, trying to look as casual as possible. He

found himself fussing with his own short, brown hair a bit. It gave him something to do with his hands and hopefully made him look less awkward. "Oh," he said. "Hey, Duke."

"What's with all the books?" Duke said as Billy walked up behind him.

"Hey, Simon," Billy said.

"Books? Oh, these? Oh . . . nothing," Kevin said in an almost stutter.

"What, your parents got you studying all summer?" Duke said. He was still staring at the stack of novels.

"What? No," Kevin said. Then he thought better of it. "Yeah," he said. "They got me on a summer reading thing. Because of what happened." Kevin didn't like to lie, but Duke had handed him an excuse on a silver platter. It would be a waste not to use it.

"Sucks, man," Duke said. "They can't even get me to do the reading for school. I just watch the movie. That way I do all right on the tests."

"Huh," Kevin said.

He was thinking to himself about all the good books Duke was missing out on. Some of his favorite novels had been turned into movies, and the films themselves never seemed quite as good. But instead he said, "Maybe I'll try that."

"Kevin?" came his mom's voice from behind him. She didn't sound happy. "What's going on?"

Duke and Billy didn't even turn to look at her. They simply hopped on their boards and kicked off back toward the gazebo.

"Check you later, man," Duke said. Billy smiled and nodded at Kevin.

Kevin turned to see his mom's disapproving look. It was the same face she made when he came home with his first skateboard. It was not a look that Kevin enjoyed.

"Let's go," she said. She pushed the button on her keychain and unlocked the SUV. Then she walked around to the driver's side. Kevin got into the passenger's seat. At least that was over. Now all he had to worry about was a nice, warm summer and a stack of promising books.

His mom waited until they were a few blocks away to start talking. "So, I solved your problem," she said.

"Huh?" Kevin said.

"About what you're going to do this summer," she said.

Kevin wouldn't actually call that a problem. But before he could tell his mom that, she was talking again.

"I spoke to Mr. Belmont. I thought he might need some help around his place, and I was right. He does need someone to work on his place," she said. "I don't know if you've been by there, but it's an absolute mess. You should see the yard."

This doesn't sound good, thought Kevin.

"So you start Monday," his mom said. "You'll mow the grass, pull weeds, straighten up inside. Whatever Mr. Belmont needs. And before you ask, no, you won't be getting paid."

Definitely not good.

"Congratulations, Kevin," his mom said. "You've just earned yourself your first summer job."

And there it was. The other shoe had finally dropped.

#
THE BARN

Kevin looked behind him as he walked. He wanted to make sure no one could see him from the house. It was a long way to the barn, and he really didn't want his mom or dad to see where he was going. The last thing he needed was to be interrupted.

Luckily, there was no one in sight. There was just a long stretch of green grass in front of him, and the same thing behind. It wasn't a surprise. His parents rarely came out here. Ever since they'd moved to Ohio when Kevin was a baby, the barn had been used as nothing more than a very large and very old storage unit.

The wooden door creaked on its rails as Kevin slid it open. He could see dust swirling in the light of the afternoon sun. The barn wasn't exactly the cleanest place on their property. In fact, it was what his mom often called "a real eyesore." The concrete floor that ran the length of the building was cracked in dozens of spots. It even had a few chunks missing here and there. The roof was spotted with jagged holes. The neighborhood birds seemed to think those holes were some sort of invitation to come in and build nests.

Old farm equipment that hadn't been used in decades crowded the large main room. The place was so packed, it had taken Kevin the better part of three weeks to even clear a decent-sized path through the cluttered space. But the family's driveway was gravel and led out onto two steep hills in either direction. So this was the only place around for miles for Kevin to do what he loved best.

He walked over to a broken-down lawn mower covered with a tarp. Folding the tarp back a little, he smiled. His skateboard sat there, waiting for him. Kevin picked it up by its tail and dusted it off. He loved his board, even if it wasn't as tricked out as Duke's or as expensive as Billy's.

Kevin's board was simple. It had a black deck lined in grip tape, a red metallic finish underneath, and bright-blue wheels. It wasn't coated in stickers or graffiti. It was neat and clean.

The board coasted on the uneven floor with Kevin gracefully balanced on top of it. He skated over to the door of the barn. He'd forgotten to close it, and he certainly didn't need his parents to catch him skating there. They weren't exactly fans of the sport. In fact, if skateboarding hadn't been Kevin's only real form of exercise, he figured they would have taken his board away by now. Either way, he was sure he'd get in trouble if they found him skating around all of the machinery.

With the barn door tightly shut, Kevin was back on his board. He circled the floor a few times as a warm up. The fourth time around, he popped an ollie. The next time around he tried a switch ollie and landed just as easily. He glided across the dusty floor, dodging cracks and holes. Kevin tended to be a bit clumsy off his board, but on it, he was just the opposite. Besides school, this was the one thing he was really good at.

He took a deep breath as he started another loop. Confined there on his small makeshift path, Kevin's mind drifted. He thought about a day when he would leave this small town behind him. He'd head to a big city with skateparks and sidewalks. There'd be plenty of handrails to grind and new tricks to try. There would be people just like him who wouldn't make him feel bad for liking what he happened to like.

But most importantly, in the big city there wouldn't be grumpy, old neighbors with gigantic overgrown lawns that needed to be mowed all summer long.

THE FIRST DAY

"You can sigh all you want, but it's not going to change anything," Kevin's mom said as she pulled the car into Mr. Belmont's lane.

Kevin looked away from her and rolled his eyes.

"This will be good for you," she said. "Now put on a happy face. Look, there's Mr. Belmont now."

The car came to a stop at the top of the lane. Kevin stepped out of the SUV and into the shadow of Mr. Belmont's large house. He looked at the chipped walls and dirty windows. He looked at the overgrown grass of the yard that lined the driveway. The weeds were nearly up to his waist. Then he looked over at the front entrance to the house.

There stood Mr. Belmont. The old man's face looked as unwelcoming as his property.

"Good to see you again, Mr. Belmont," Kevin's mom called over to the old man. She was still sitting in the SUV, ready to head to town on her errands.

Mr. Belmont simply nodded his head at Kevin's mom. It looked like he almost smiled, but Kevin couldn't be sure. Smiling didn't seem like something Mr. Belmont liked to do that often.

As Kevin's mom backed out of the lane, Mr. Belmont walked over to Kevin. He looked down at him without saying a word.

Feeling more awkward than usual, Kevin said, "Um. Hello."

Mr. Belmont grunted. Then he walked past Kevin toward a stone path that led to the backyard. Kevin stayed where he was. After he'd walked a few yards, Mr. Belmont stopped and turned back to face his new employee. "Well, come on then," he said.

Kevin followed Mr. Belmont through the path, noticing that the grass all around him seemed to be getting taller as they went. Mr. Belmont didn't mention the overgrowth. Instead, he led Kevin to a small toolshed. He opened the door to reveal an outdated push lawn mower, a rake, and a rusted wheelbarrow.

"Start with the side yard," the old man said. "Mow. Rake. Dump the grass out back. Nothing to it."

Kevin studied the equipment in front of him. "So, where exactly should I —" he started to say before realizing that he was talking to himself. Mr. Belmont was already halfway back down the path, heading to the back door of the house.

"Okay then," Kevin said under his breath. There was nothing left to do but get to work.

* * *

Two hours later, Kevin had only managed to cut a small portion of the side yard. The grass was too thick for Kevin to work any faster. At one point, he'd almost knocked over a birdbath that he couldn't see in all the weeds. It was only ten in the morning, and he was already exhausted. He couldn't

imagine what it would be like soon when the sun really started to beat down on him.

Kevin wiped the sweat from his forehead. He could use some ice water or something. He debated knocking on the back door of the house. But then he noticed something on the stoop. He walked over closer towards the cracked, old steps and saw a freshly poured glass of lemonade waiting for him. He picked up the glass, feeling the cold condensation against his hand. Then he walked to a shady patch under a nearby tree and took a drink.

From where he was standing, Kevin could see one of the upstairs windows of the house. There were several facing this side of the yard, but only one of the windows didn't have its curtains drawn. After a moment or two, there was movement in the window. Mr. Belmont was walking across the room. He stopped and looked down at Kevin. Politely, Kevin smiled and waved up at the old man. Mr. Belmont didn't react at first. Then he just nodded his head at Kevin and continued on his way.

Kevin shrugged and finished his lemonade. Then he picked up the rickety, old rake and walked over to the patch of grass that he had already mowed. The grass was so long that after only a few minutes of raking, he had a pile large enough to fill the wheelbarrow. And after loading up the mud-caked old thing, Kevin pushed it further down the stone path toward the back of the house.

Even though the woods behind Kevin's house connected to the woods behind Mr. Belmont's house, Kevin had never seen Mr. Belmont's backyard. He figured there were very few people who had.

The backyard was as overgrown as the front, so Kevin wasn't sure where he was supposed to dump the mowed grass. He decided to make a pile in the woods that lined the yard's far end, but getting there was proving to be a problem. The wheelbarrow was heavy and hard to steer. Just as Kevin thought he was getting the hang of it, the front tire slid off the bumpy stone path. Kevin couldn't hold on. Before he knew it, the entire wheelbarrow had overturned with him underneath it.

With a bit of effort, Kevin pushed the heavy thing off of himself. He stood up and looked around the yard. He was more than a little annoyed that he'd have to collect the grass again. But then he noticed another stone path connecting to the one he was standing on. It was narrower than the first, and quite curvy. Curious, Kevin decided to take a five-minute break and see where this trail led him.

The path wound around a few large trees. Kevin followed it as overgrown weeds brushed against his arms and legs. Then suddenly, the stones beneath his feet became flat concrete. There was a staircase in front of Kevin, decorated with a slightly rusty handrail. Kevin climbed the steps. When he got to the top, he gasped. What he saw in front of him was so impressive he couldn't help but react.

There, at the top of the hill, was an empty swimming pool. It had a rounded bottom, handrails leading down steps, and even wave-like bumps on its floor that looked almost like moguls on a ski slope. It snaked around the hilltop and seemed to go on forever.

Trees shaded its sides, and leaves covered the empty bottom. A few stone benches decorated the edges here and there, and some of the concrete outside the pool was shaped into little wave-like hills as well. Like the rest of Mr. Belmont's property, the pool needed a lot of help. But if he worked

hard enough on it, in just a few days Kevin was sure he could transform it into the most amazing skatepark he'd ever seen. A skatepark that was pretty much right in his own backyard.

SECRET SKATEPARK

For ten days straight, Kevin worked through lunch and stayed at Mr. Belmont's until dark. Kevin's parents were proud of his work ethic, but they had no idea what he was really doing with all those extra hours.

Mr. Belmont didn't either, in fact. The old man couldn't see the pool from his house, so he had no way of knowing that Kevin was staying on his property two to three hours longer each afternoon. Kevin had told him that he was just going to walk home through the woods. And while that statement wasn't exactly true, it wasn't exactly a lie, either. Kevin did walk home that way. He just did it after he'd spent a few hours shoveling leaves out from the bottom of the pool, or trimming the overgrowth around the stone benches.

Now all that hard work was about to pay off. Kevin stood on the edge of the pool with one of his feet balanced on his skateboard. In front of him stretched the winding pool with its curved sides and mogul-lined base. This was it. The moment he'd been waiting for. He kicked off gently and placed both feet squarely on his board's deck.

And then he flew.

Dropping in, Kevin and his skateboard glided down the pool's slope. He shifted his weight to skate around the round side. The wind whipped against his face and blew his hair out of place. He cruised to the bottom of the pool and hit his first mogul. He caught a little air, but landed perfectly.

The maneuver had slowed him down a bit, so he pushed against the concrete below him when he had the chance. His board raced across the pool's floor and up the far side. He grinded around the lip of the pool before heading back down the slope. He circled the pool once more and then tried a grind off the handrail by the steps. And even though he lost his balance and fell to the concrete without his board, Kevin

grinned. He stood up and looked around. He wasn't just cruising around a small, dusty loop in his barn any longer.

No, Kevin Simon was now the custodian and sole user of his own secret skatepark.

SOMEONE NEW

The next afternoon, Kevin wasn't particularly focused on what he was doing. He honestly didn't feel that the day's task deserved that much thought. He was simply carrying boxes from a room upstairs in Mr. Belmont's home to his already crowded basement. It was a job a trained monkey could do.

So Kevin thought it better to put his mind to work on other projects. At the moment, he was busy trying to figure out the best way to construct a ramp for his skatepark. It was really the only thing missing. He could obtain some air from the moguls, but not really enough to do a decent McTwist or anything.

If Kevin had been paying attention to what he was doing, he might have noticed the tape on the bottom of the box he was carrying. He might have detected how it had yellowed with age and was peeling at the sides. And he might have realized that this particular piece of tape might not be quite as sticky as it used to be.

The box gave out just as Kevin reached the top of the stairs leading down to the basement. A waterfall of picture frames and books poured out onto the steps below. The sound of shattering glass grabbed Kevin's attention at last.

Kevin walked down the stairs carrying the empty, broken box. He surveyed the damage on the floor below him. There were a few broken picture frames, a couple of photo albums, and what looked like several trophies and plaques. He picked the closest and largest trophy off the ground. Luckily, it hadn't been damaged in the fall. He studied the engraved letters on its base. It read: 1953 Soap Box Derby – 2nd Place.

"Ahem," said a voice behind him. Apparently, the shattering glass had gotten more than just Kevin's attention.

Kevin turned around to see Mr. Belmont standing on the

lowest stair. Mr. Belmont's loafers stepped down onto the basement floor. He walked over toward Kevin.

"I'm sorry, sir," Kevin said in a bit of a panic. "The box broke, and I wasn't able to . . ."

"That one's from 1953," Mr. Belmont interrupted.

Kevin looked down at the trophy again.

"Should have had that one, but the Thompkins kid beat me by a nose," Mr. Belmont said. "Or that's what the judges said. Still don't know if I believe them."

Kevin didn't say anything. He was pretty sure that Mr. Belmont had just spoken more words than he'd heard him say all summer.

"You ever race a soap box?" Mr. Belmont said, looking at Kevin.

Kevin shook his head no. Mr. Belmont walked over to one of the shattered picture frames and picked it up. He shook the remainder of the broken glass out of the frame. Then he pointed the picture toward Kevin so he could see it. It was a black-and-white photo of a young boy proudly sitting in a sleek-looking miniature racecar. There was a big nine painted in a circle on the car's side.

"That was me," Mr. Belmont said. "Not sure what year this one's from. That was at the World Championship. Used to have it over in Akron."

"So you built the car yourself?" asked Kevin.

"Yep. With the help of a buddy of mine," said Mr. Belmont. "The trick with a soap box car is you can't have a motor. The thing's gotta be powered by nothing but gravity. You got to know what you're doing because come race time, it's more you than the car."

"Did you win?" Kevin asked.

"No, didn't even place," said Mr. Belmont. "Had a loose wheel that time. I lost control and crashed into an old woman eating an ice cream cone."

Kevin laughed. He didn't mean to. He wasn't sure if this was a sore subject or not.

But now Mr. Belmont was smiling, too. "Lady yelled at me for what must have been something like five minutes straight. She got ice cream all over her favorite dress and ruined it." Mr. Belmont laughed while thinking about it. "I said, 'Lady, you're the one who ordered black cherry ice cream. If you'd ordered vanilla, we wouldn't be in this mess.'"

Kevin laughed again. Up until now it had seemed impossible that Mr. Belmont had ever been a day younger than sixty-five in his entire life. This happy old man in front of him was someone new altogether.

Mr. Belmont walked to the corner of the room where a few brooms and mops hung from hooks on the wall. He took two brooms down and handed one to Kevin.

"Help me with this, will ya?" he asked as he started to sweep up the glass from one of the frames. Kevin walked over to where two other pictures had shattered and started to do the same. Neither said anything for a few moments. But then Mr. Belmont was talking again.

"Of course that wasn't my worst wreck," he said. "That one was in 1957, I think. Just a practice run down the hill there on Cobblestone by Main Street. That one was a sight to see."

"Yeah?" said Kevin.

It took the two of them about five minutes to sweep up the glass and fix the box. But they stayed down there talking for the next half hour.

THE SECRET'S OUT

Kevin skidded down the concrete slope. He stood up and looked at his knee. It wasn't too bad. It was just scraped a little. He'd lost his balance and concentration for a minute, and it had cost him. He walked over to the center of Mr. Belmont's pool and picked up his board. Time to try that nosestall again.

As he walked up the steps to the edge of the pool, he noticed how dark it was getting. The sun had started going down about an hour ago. Kevin swatted at what seemed like the fiftieth mosquito that had thought his arm was a good place for an evening snack. He was going to get eaten alive by bugs if he stayed there much longer. He hadn't gotten much skating in the day before since he and Mr. Belmont had been swapping stories. So he was trying to make up some time in his skatepark tonight. But if he didn't get home soon, dodging mosquitoes would be the least of his worries. Finding an excuse to tell his mom would be the real challenge.

Kevin walked over to the small bathhouse that neighbored the pool. The structure had seen better days, even when compared to some of the still overgrown sections of the yard. Kevin propped his board up on the wall right inside the small building's front door. He'd like to fix up the bathhouse, too. All it needed was some sweeping, cleaning, and a few chairs. Then it would be the perfect place to get some shade and do a little reading.

With his board safely hidden away, he shut the door behind him and headed towards the woods. But right when he crossed the tree line, he heard a very familiar sound. It was a high-pitched cackle. And it was coming from Mr. Belmont's front yard.

It was completely dark now. There wasn't much of a moon out tonight, so it was hard for Kevin to navigate. But at this point, he knew Mr. Belmont's property pretty well. So he was able to sneak around to the front yard without making much noise. He stayed close to the house for cover. Then he peered around the building's corner to see what was going on.

Duke and Billy were standing there near the road. While most people probably couldn't make them out from that distance in the dark, Kevin could spot Duke's pale skin and hair pretty easily. Duke was holding a roll of toilet paper in his hand and moving it back and forth. He was preparing to throw it into the tree above him, but he was taking time with his aim. Billy had been tasked with holding the large pack of toilet paper.

Over near the road were two bikes with backpacks piled next to them. The two kids were ready for a quick getaway should Mr. Belmont catch them in the act. As Duke threw the roll of paper into the tree, Kevin thought about Mr. Belmont. He thought about how tomorrow was his day off. Mr. Belmont would have to clean up this mess all by himself.

Kevin sighed and then stepped out from the house. He jogged over to Billy and Duke.

"Hey, whoa . . ." Billy said as he saw Kevin running

toward him. He seemed worried that they were about to be caught. But when he saw who it was, he relaxed. "Oh, hey, man," he said.

Duke looked over his shoulder and stopped what he was doing. "Huh?" he said. And then added, "Simon. What up, man?"

"How'd you know we were here?" asked Billy.

"I was in the back. I'm working for Mr. Belmont this summer," he said.

"Sick, man," said Duke. "You have to clean up after the old man?"

"Well . . . yeah. Kind of," said Kevin.

"That sucks," said Billy.

"Yeah, especially after tonight," said Duke. "You are gonna have one heck of a mess on your hands. You know it's gonna rain tomorrow?"

"Um, I guess," Kevin said.

"Yeah, and wait'll you see what rain does to this stuff," Duke said through a wide smile. He threw his roll of toilet paper at the tree above him. "Old man's gonna be picking scraps of TP out of his trees for months."

"Guys, come on," said Kevin. He was trying to think of a way to say what he had to say without making them think he was some sort of baby. "Can't you toilet paper somebody else's place? I'm going to have to clean this up," Kevin said.

"Nah, dude," said Duke. "Old guy keeps yelling at us when we're skating at the library. Like he owns the place. This is payback."

Billy was smiling, going along with another of Duke's schemes.

"He'll know it was you," Kevin said.

"So?" said Duke.

"So he knows I'm friends with you guys. I'll get fired," Kevin said. "I've got a pretty good thing going here and . . ."

"This is a pretty good thing? You cleanin' up some old dude's crap all summer is a good thing? It sucks, dude," Duke said. "We're doing you a favor, and you know it."

Kevin's thought for a second, and then said, "Fine." He turned away from them and added, "I guess I'll just show you."

"What? You gonna turn us in to your new grandpa?" Duke said.

"Just come on," Kevin said again, waving with his hand for them to follow him.

Billy dropped the large package of toilet paper and headed after Kevin. Duke trailed behind them at a safe distance. He wasn't sure if he could totally trust Kevin. He even took his backpack with him so he was ready for a quick getaway.

Kevin led the two boys around the side yard and down the stone path. He paused for a second there in the dark. But he didn't see any other way out of his situation. So he reluctantly trudged up the hill. And in a matter of seconds, his secret skatepark was no longer a secret.

LEAVE YOUR MARK

Once Billy and Duke got over their initial awe, they immediately had to try out the pool. Since Kevin had the only board at the moment, they all took turns on the waves, the rails, and the rounded slopes. It was fun for Kevin to see the guys again, but he kept having to quiet them down. Billy and Duke weren't Mr. Belmont's favorite people, and Kevin hated the idea of getting caught with them. A half hour passed before Kevin decided that the party had to be cut short.

"Guys," he said. "I've got to get back. My mom's going to freak as it is."

"Aw, man," said Duke. He was standing at the top of the pool, watching Billy skate in his usual goofy-foot style. "You can't leave until we personalize the place a little."

Kevin didn't like the sound of that.

Duke pulled a familiar can of red spray paint out of his bag. "Gotta leave your mark," Duke said.

Kevin watched as Duke jumped down into the pool, shaking the can the whole time. He didn't say anything as Duke sprayed a stylized D onto the concrete side and drew a circle around it. It was the same crude tag he always used. Since Billy was still skating, Duke tossed the can up to Kevin.

"You're up, Simon," Duke said.

"I gotta get home, man," Kevin said.

"What, you get caught once so now you're chicken?" Duke said. He smiled back at Billy for support, but Billy was busy just trying to stay on his board. The moguls were trickier than they looked. "It's all part of the game, Simon."

Kevin wasn't sure that Duke's game was one he wanted to play. But even still, he found himself jumping down into the pool just the same. It wouldn't be a big deal, Kevin told himself. Mr. Belmont never went up to the pool, anyway. He had no idea that Kevin had even cleaned it up. He wouldn't notice a few tags here and there.

The can rattled in Kevin's hand as he shook it, scaring

away another mosquito at the same time. Kevin didn't even know what he was going to draw. A K might be too obvious if Mr. Belmont did ever come up here. He'd have to think of something.

"What are you doing there?" a voice yelled behind Kevin.

Kevin turned around and saw Mr. Belmont standing on the opposite side of the pool. Billy had apparently seen the old man a few seconds earlier. In fact, he had already disappeared into the woods. And Duke was right behind him. If Kevin wasn't busy feeling so guilty, he'd have noticed an unmistakable sensation of déjà vu.

Mr. Belmont yelled after Billy and Duke. Then he turned to look down at Kevin. It seemed like it took him a second to recognize Kevin standing there in the darkness. And when he did, Kevin watched as Mr. Belmont's face changed from anger to an even more upsetting expression. He looked disappointed.

Kevin didn't say anything. He just dropped the spray can on the ground, and ran into the woods.

MESSED UP

A hyena-like, high-pitched cackle echoed through the patch of dense trees. As Kevin got closer to it, he saw Duke and Billy laughing with one another.

Duke was leaning back against a tree, saying, "That guy was so mad."

"How are we gonna get our bikes?" Billy asked through his big grin.

"We've got to double back quick before he calls the cops or something," said Duke. The two looked like they were about to do just that when Kevin finally caught up to them. When he saw his friend, Duke stopped and said, "Awesome. You got away this time."

Kevin didn't answer.

"Dude, that place is seriously great," said Duke. "I know what you were talking about now. We'll come back tomorrow night. But this time, we'll all bring boards."

Kevin looked at Billy, and then back at Duke. All three kids were out of breath from running, and no one said anything for a second.

Then Kevin said, "No. You're not going back."

"We need to get our bikes," Duke said. "Stop being such a baby."

"I'm not talking about tonight," said Kevin. "You're not going back to the pool. Ever."

"Oh, just because you found it. That makes it your property?" said Duke as he rolled his eyes.

"No, it's Mr. Belmont's property. And we need to respect that. I shouldn't have shown it to you in the first place," Kevin said. He was angry now. And his voice was making that clear.

"Whatever, man. You been skating there for weeks. You said so yourself. I bet the old man wouldn't be happy about that, either. Now we can't go there just because you say so?"

Duke's voice sounded almost as angry as Kevin's. It was certainly getting more high-pitched.

"You're right," Kevin said. "I should have asked him. But I didn't, and now everything's messed up."

"Don't try to put this all on me," said Duke. "You were gonna tag that wall just like I did. You ain't all Mr. Innocent all of the sudden."

"That doesn't change what I said. You're not going back there," Kevin said. He moved closer to Duke and looked down at him. Kevin was barely taller than him, but it didn't seem that way right now. Still, Duke didn't back down. He had Billy for support. In Duke's eyes, it was two against one. Kevin was outnumbered. But when Duke looked over at his sidekick, Billy was looking away. He wouldn't even make eye contact with his friend.

Duke looked back into Kevin's eyes, trying to look as tough as possible. Neither moved for a few seconds. And then Duke turned away. His blond hair smacked Kevin in the face a little bit as he moved.

"Fine," he said. "Whatever, man. Keep the place to yourself. See if we care. We gotta go get our bikes."

Kevin watched as Duke disappeared into the forest. Billy followed him. But when he was a few yards away, he stopped and turned back. "See ya, Kev," he said. Then Billy turned around again and hustled after his old friend.

A mosquito landed on Kevin's arm. He smashed it and wiped his hand on his shorts. Then he turned to head home. He wasn't looking forward to the conversation he was about to have with his parents.

SETTING THINGS RIGHT

Kevin rang the doorbell again, just as he had every morning for the last week. There was still no answer. He had been coming back to Mr. Belmont's house every day at this time in the hopes of apologizing to his old boss. He knew he was fired for what had happened the other night, but he at least wanted to let the old man know that he was really and truly sorry that he had done it. He waited five minutes, but there was still no answer. So it was a good thing that Kevin had come prepared today.

He flung his book bag over his shoulder and headed to the backyard. He walked up the stone path and up the hill to the swimming pool. Then he jumped down onto its concrete

floor. He unzipped his bag and pulled a large can of paint thinner from it. Then he started splashing the liquid onto the side of the pool on the stylized red D.

The internet article Kevin found about removing spray paint had said to wait for thirty minutes for the concrete to absorb the paint thinner. He figured that as long as he was waiting, he might as well do some work around the yard.

The first thing he did was get rid of all the scraps of toilet paper still left in the trees in the front yard. After that, he gave the side yard a trim with the lawn mower, and then he moved on to the front yard. Kevin thought he'd start on a particularly overgrown patch on the far side of the house. By the time he headed back to the pool to scrub the wall, the day had gone by and the sun was setting.

With the help of a little more paint thinner, Kevin was able to get most of the paint off the pool wall. Done for the day, he stood at the pool's edge and thought about how this would normally be when he would do a bit of skating. He looked across the yard and saw his board. It was resting in the grass under the stone bench, right where Billy had dropped it when he took off running.

Kevin thought about walking around to pick the board up and take it home. And then he decided it could wait. Instead, he walked around the pool in the other direction, heading toward the woods.

On his way, the gleam of sunlight on glass caught Kevin's attention. He turned to look at the stoop at the back of the house. There on the top step was a glass of lemonade waiting for him. He walked over to it and picked up the cold glass. Then he walked over beneath the nearby tree and looked up at the window with the open curtains. Mr. Belmont was up there, looking down at him. He didn't wave or smile. He just nodded. And then he walked away and out of sight.

Kevin waved up at the window and called, "See you tomorrow morning!"

Then he turned toward the woods and headed for home.

It took a few months, but Kevin Simon finally proved to Mr. Belmont that he could be trusted. Now the two of them enjoy their cold lemonade in the newly cleaned-out poolhouse.

2S Strong

L2S Simon Hawk Face

L2S Belmont Soap Box

SKATE CLINIC:
NOSESTALL

1. As you skate up to the top of the ramp, roll into a nose manual, skating on just the front wheels. You'll have to lean toward the coping as you near it.

2. Just before your front wheels ride off the top of the ramp, push down on your front foot so that you catch the coping between the nose and the front truck.

3. Pressing the nose of the board down, hang at the edge of the ramp for a moment.

4. Drop back in.

SKATE CLINIC:
TERMS

crooked grind
a move where the skater grinds a rail or edge with the front truck of the board while angling the tail of the board away from the rail or edge so that the board's nose also rubs along the edge

dropping in
placing the board on the edge of a ramp and riding down

grind
a move in which one or both trucks slide across the surface of an object

nosestall
a move where the skater reaches the top of the transition, leans on the skateboard's nose atop the ramp, and drops back in

ollie
a move where the rider pops the skateboard into the air with his or her feet

switch ollie
an ollie that is done with the rider's less preferred foot at the front of the board

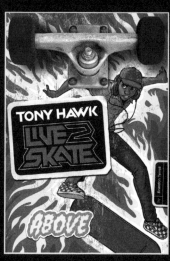

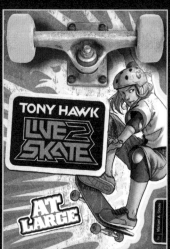

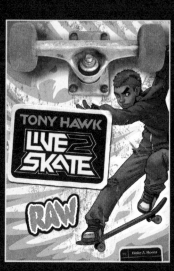

HOW DO YOU LIVE?

written by
MATTHEW K. MANNING

Matthew K. Manning is a comic book writer, historian, and fan. Over the course of his career, he's written comics or books starring Batman, Superman, Iron Man, Wolverine, Captain America, Thor, Spider-Man, the Incredible Hulk, the Flash, the Legion of Super-Heroes, the Justice League, and even Bugs Bunny. Some of his more recent works include the popular hardcover for Andrews McMeel Publishing entitled *The Batman Files* and an upcoming creator-owned, six-issue miniseries for DC Comics. He lives in Mystic, Connecticut, with his wife Dorothy and daughter Lillian.

pencils and colors by
FERNANDO CANO

Fernando Cano is an all-around artist living in Monterrey, Mexico, currently working as a concept artist for video game company CGbot. Having published with Marvel, DC, Pathfinder, and IDW, he spends his free time playing video games, singing, writing, and above all, drawing!

inks by
JOE AZPEYTIA

Joe Azpeytia currently lives in Mexico and works as a freelance graphic designer for music bands and international companies. Currently an illustration artist at The Door on the Wall studio, he enjoys playing drums, playing video games, and drawing.